THE
GAMBLE

BARE KNUCKLE

THE GAMBLE

PATRICK JONES

darbycreek

MINNEAPOLIS

Darby Creek
A division of Lerner Publishing Group, Inc.
241 First Avenue North
Minneapolis, MN 55401 U.S.A.

Website address: www.lernerbooks.com

Cover and interior photographs © iStockphoto.com/Steve Krumenaker (brick background); © iStockphoto.com/tomograf (paper texture); © iStockphoto.com/ Abomb Industries Design (woodrat); © iStockphoto.com/CSA_Images (fist).

For reading levels and more information, look up this title at www.lernerbooks.com.

Main body text set in Janson Text LT Std 12/17.
Typeface provided by Linotype AG.

Library of Congress Cataloging-in-Publication Data

Jones, Patrick, 1961–
        The gamble / by Patrick Jones.
            pages   cm. — (Bareknuckle)
        Summary: In nineteenth-century New York City, teenaged Leung promises not to compete in bareknuckle boxing matches until he fixes his sloppy technique, but when his uncle's gambling debts get out of control, Leung must enter the ring to save him.
        ISBN 978–1–4677–1462–4 (lib. bdg. : alk. paper)
        ISBN 978–1–4677–2410–4 (eBook)
        [1. Boxing—Fiction. 2. Immigrants—Fiction. 3. Chinese Americans—Fiction. 4. Orphans—Fiction. 5. Uncles—Fiction. 6. New York (N.Y.)—History—1865–1898—Fiction.] I. Title.
        PZ7.J7242Gam 2014
        [Fic]—dc23   2013027522

Manufactured in the United States of America
1 – SB – 12/31/13

NEW YORK CITY.
THE 1870s.
THE FIGHT STARTS NOW.

CHAPTER ONE

"Center yourself!" Uncle Tso slapped Leung's legs with a bamboo rod to make the point. Leung said nothing as the thick stick snapped against his hamstrings.

Uncle Tso raised himself from the wooden stool he'd brought into the alley. Leung and his uncle were training behind the crowded Mott Street tenement that they now called home.

Tso placed his right hand on Leung's shoulders and whispered, "Be like bamboo: firm yet flexible. Centered but supple."

Tso spoke the words in Chinese. He had refused to learn English since they crossed the country five years back, from California to New York, riding the rails their family had helped to build.

Leung drew in a deep breath and vowed to find the perfect balance within himself. Late-spring dew hung heavy in the air, but it would soon surrender to the smells of a lower Manhattan morning. From each of the Five Points— from the Italians, the Irish, and now the Chinese—came scents of breakfasts cooked and beverages brewed.

"If balanced, you can both attack and defend. Balance is the essence of Wing Chun," Uncle Tso explained. Leung stared at his foe: a wooden dummy. Tso had mastered wooden dummy combat, yet he rarely did so well against human foes. Unlike Leung's father. His father had won every battle from California to Utah and back again. And unlike the burly bareknuckle boxers Leung had spied battling at the Woodrat Club, Leung's father had fought for pride, not for pennies.

"Leung, keep a high narrow stance. Hold your elbows close," his uncle explained, his voice strong yet soft. "Your arms protect your body."

With his elbows tucked tight, Leung threw hard strikes with his hands and then his feet. The first rule of fighting was to protect yourself—Leung's father had once said this. The man had lived that way; he had died that way too.

Leung corrected his stance and threw faster, more accurate punches against the dummy. "Your form must be perfect," Uncle Tso said. "Leave nothing to chance."

Biting on his bottom lip, Leung held back a chuckle. Chance? Uncle Tso's life revolved around games of chance. To Leung's knowledge, Tso had yet to venture into white gambling dens, but he was well known in the parlors of Chinatown, often disappearing for days.

"Is something funny?" Uncle Tso snapped the rod near Leung's bare feet.

Leung shook his head. Sweat dripped down his bare chest. "I want to fight, not just practice forms," he muttered.

"You have no challengers here," Tso replied. "Few here know Wing Chun, and none are better."

"Then across Mott Street. There are fights at the Woodrat, and I—"

Uncle Tso ended Leung's sentence with a smack of the stick across his face. "No."

Leung ran his hands over his shaved head. A long, black strand of hair hung behind him, as was custom for young Chinese men. Traces of blood from his hands turned his sweat crimson.

Uncle Tso resumed his instructions: "Center yourself. Breathe in. Relax. Punch with your body, not your arms. Don't punch straight, but up. Punch up and—"

"Your foe goes down," Leung said.

CHAPTER TWO

"Do it again, Leung," Uncle Nang snapped in Chinese. When Uncle Nang taught the older students, he spoke English. Except when he was angry.

Leung reasoned through the math problem again. He believed that when the chance came, he could defeat any man in a fight, but the abacus was an unbeatable foe.

Leung's Uncle Tso and his father had taught him the art of Wing Chun. But Uncle Nang, his father's oldest brother, taught him everything else. It was Uncle Nang who left Guangdong, their province by the South China Sea, for America in 1850.

Although Nang never found gold in California, he believed he'd found a place of more opportunities than he had ever known in China. Leung, his father, other uncles, and nephews arrived five years later. Most of the woman stayed behind, although Leung's mother joined them on the journey. She had died while on the trip.

"Let me see your hands!" Uncle Nang said. Leung complied. The knuckles were scraped, cut, and bruised, just the way Leung liked them. Uncle Nang shook his head.

"Why does Tso continue to waste your time?" Nang continued.

"He wants me to be the fighter he never was," Leung said, replying to Nang in their native tongue.

"English!" Uncle Nang shouted at the class, and maybe to remind himself of his own rules. The other students—twenty in total, ranging in age from seven to Leung's seventeen—whispered and giggled. "If we are to succeed, we must learn their language. We must learn and obey their rules."

"They don't obey their own rules," Leung said. "That is why my father is dead."

Nang nodded and walked away. After the riot in California that took his brother's life, Nang had moved the family to New York. It wasn't the paradise he had imagined. Instead, he and the others were cold, hungry, and jammed together in small spaces.

The Five Points offered few places for the children to play and no place but the alley for Leung to practice Wing Chun. None of the residents of the neighborhood practiced the form, which made no sense to Leung. Didn't they know what had happened in California? Why didn't they learn how to protect their families? For Tso, safety came by avoiding contact with the white world; for Leung, the best protection was to show everyone that he was a fighting master.

"You have nothing to say, Uncle Nang?"

Leung asked. Nang never spoke of his brother's death.

Uncle Nang said nothing in Chinese or in English. Leung tensed his arms, holding back the urge to strike out. Finally, Uncle Nang spoke. "America is a hard land."

Leung turned his attention back to the abacus. His uncle began to work with younger students. Because Nang spoke some English, he'd been a valuable man not just to his family but to all the other Chinese working on the railroad. Valuable, but not strong or brave enough to save his brother's life.

As other students chattered on, Leung again heard Uncle Nang say something about obeying the rules. But those rules had done nothing to protect their family five years ago, when the rioters came. Leung had just started to learn Wing Chun then, so he could do nothing as he watched his father murdered, his house burned, and his family robbed. Leung wasn't a fortune teller like those that Uncle Tso visited in the gambling parlors, but he knew the path that lay before him: vengeance.

Yet, when he felt the heat of hatred rise within him, Leung knew to stay centered. He closed his eyes and dreamed of achieving perfect form and balance.

CHAPTER THREE

"Where are you going so fast?" Uncle Tso asked Leung.

Leung knew he couldn't lie to his uncle, so he pretended not to hear him.

"Leung!"

Uncle Tso reached out and grabbed Leung's arm with this right hand, but Leung escaped his uncle's grasp. "I have to go," was all Leung said before he ran toward Mott Street.

The tiny street overflowed with other Chinese immigrants. As Leung walked down the crowded street, he passed the sidewalk vendors selling candy and cigars. Chinatown was its own world, but Leung longed for more.

From his back pocket, he removed the folded-up scrap of paper that he'd come across the night before, when he'd ventured into the Five Points. Like Leung's neighborhood, the Five Points was filled with old buildings jammed with people new to the city. Leung suspected that as bad as things were in the Five Points, everyone had come there to escape something worse. Before Leung took the step across Mott toward Mulberry, he put on a large straw hat to hide his features.

He walked head down, clutching the paper. It showed a drawing of two men posing with their elbows bent. Leung didn't need to read English to know what it meant: a bareknuckle fight at the Woodrat.

The club was to the east, in the Bowery. It wasn't Leung's first time sneaking out to peek in on a fight there, but it was his first time at night. He'd overheard men say the fights at night were better, although Leung wondered how that could be. The fights he'd seen before had been bloody affairs. Men lost teeth, and in one case, a man had his eye knocked out of its socket. Brutal affairs, long on brawn but short on brains. Fighters without fear or form.

To Leung's disappointment, a crowd of drunks stood in front of the tiny window he'd peered through before. Leung knew better than to try to go inside.

Leung walked past the crowd, through the garbage-packed ally. Men began shouting and clapping from inside the club as if the fight were about to begin. Leung piled wooden crates on top of other crates to form a makeshift ladder. Using all his strength, he pulled himself through the window of an abandoned room above the club. As he'd hoped, a crack in the floor gave him a glimpse of the battles below.

Unsure of his footing, Leung crawled on his hands and his knees toward the best seat in the house. He gazed down in amazement as two men fought—or boxed, as men in the Bowery called it. One fighter was a young man with thick, black hair. The other was a little older, with hair the color of a carrot.

The two men punched each other until both were bleeding. Men from the crowd called out for more. Yet over all the noise, Leung heard something else, something behind him. He turned and saw a boy about his age and size, except with red hair.

"Tell me something, fella," the boy said to Leung. "Is my dad winning?"

CHAPTER FOUR

"You speak English?" the kid asked as he sat on the floor next to Leung.

Leung said nothing, but the kid kept talking. Leung struggled to understand without losing track of the fight below.

"He's undefeated, but that's 'cos it's his first fight," the kid continued.

Leung studied the form of each fighter. Neither man demonstrated balance; both men threw clumsy blows.

The boy's dad punched hard, knocking the wind out of his opponent. The other man had beaten the count so far, but Leung knew from watching his father that fighters often realize who the winner is before a fight ends.

"So, you like to watch fights?" the kid asked.

Leung shrugged.

"Me too, I want to be fighter like my dad. You fight?"

Leung shrugged again as the boy leaned in next to him.

"Is your dad teaching you? My dad's teaching me. He's a great teacher."

Leung froze but still said nothing.

"Who do you think is going to win? My dad said everyone is betting on the other guy—I guess he's from England—but let me tell you, an Irishman can beat a Brit any day of the week and twice on Sunday after church. See what I mean?"

Once again, the black-haired man below was flat on his back, except this time his eyes were closed, swelling shut. Someone threw in a white towel from the corner.

The red hair kid clapped in delight. "Ain't nobody tougher than an Irishman. Nobody on God's green earth—"

"Nobody except a Chinaman," Leung said.

The Irish kid stood up and gave Leung the once-over, as if Leung were a piece of meat in the market.

"So, you do speak. You don't speak the truth, but you speak. My name is Sean."

The kid stuck in hand out. Puzzled, Leung bowed instead.

"What, you too good to shake my hand? Or maybe you think something's wrong with me?" Sean said. "Some people don't care much for Chinamen, but I got no problem with ya."

Leung rose and centered himself, just in case. He held out his right hand but let relaxation flow through his left arm in case he needed to strike. Although his feet were planted like roots, he could swing them into action if needed.

Sean smiled as he took Leung's hand and squeezed it. "What's your name?"

Leung answered, and that made the Sean kid smile even more. Leung laughed.

"So who is tougher? An Irishman or a Chinaman?" Sean squeezed harder.

Leung squeezed back, then quickly let go. He pushed off his hat and assumed a fighting position. Cranelike, Leung stood prepared to strike.

Sean laughed. "Only a fool fights for free, with nobody watching. Are you a fool?"

Leung shook his head. Sean grabbed Leung's hat from the ground and handed it back to him.

"You got some crazy hair there, fella, and a strange way of holdin' yourself," Sean said. "It looks like—"

"It's called Wing Chun."

Sean scratched his red haired head. Leung explained the art as best he could. Mixing both English and Chinese, he shared the legend with Sean. The story of a young woman, Yim Wing-Chun, and the Buddhist nun who taught her a new way of fighting. Yim Wing-Chun used her knowledge to defeat a powerful warlord who wanted to make her his bride.

As Leung told the story, Sean laughed.

"So, you fight like a girl?" Sean asked.

"I am balanced. Graceful like the crane and dangerous like the snake." Leung didn't laugh or crack a smile as he spoke. "But I always fight like a man."

CHAPTER FIVE

"No, you're not ready," Uncle Tso scolded Leung. This session, Leung faced his uncle, not the wooden dummy. Unlike the dummy, Leung's uncle fought back.

As Leung picked himself off the pebble-filled ally, he felt pain shoot through his body. While Uncle Tso lacked striking power, he could still take Leung down with ease. Tso's perfect form allowed him to maintain his balance and throw Leung seemingly at will.

"I'm ready. I'll show you," Leung said. He threw a punch with his right hand, which his uncle blocked. Jab, kick, or throw, Leung couldn't move his uncle. In all their times sparring, Leung had never seen his uncle so balanced. Maybe Uncle Tso was right; maybe Leung wasn't ready. When would he know?

A side kick surprised Leung, but he deflected it. More arm strikes from his uncle followed, but Leung was fast enough to block each one. Leung sensed that even though they'd been sparring for just a short time, Uncle Tso was getting tired. The first fight he'd watched at the Woodrat Club had seemed to last from noon until twilight. Leung had never seen a fight of his father's last longer than the time it took to eat lunch. Did that mean boxing was better than Wing Chun? Or was it the other way around?

As Leung tried to strike back, his uncle moved in closer. Up close was where the true masters of Wing Chun were best. Although shorter than Tso, Leung was stronger. As they sparred, Leung felt he was gaining power, almost taking it from his uncle.

Uncle Tso tried a throat strike with his right hand, but Leung slipped into position behind him. Tso tried to throw Leung off, and that's when Leung felt it. His uncle's body tensed up like a board Leung could break rather than bamboo that would bend. Leung drove furious strikes to the body like his father had done to his foes, like the other workers did to the railroad spikes, until his uncle gasped and crumbled to the ground.

Leung backed off. They'd never sparred this hard before.

"How can you say I am not ready?" Leung asked.

Uncle Tso picked pebbles off his knees. He was bloody, but unbowed. He dug a finger into Leung's chest. "I say when."

"When is that?"

Breathing heavily, Uncle Tso answered. "When your form is perfect."

"But—"

"You must be graceful as the crane, but as dangerous as the snake," Tso said. "Right now you are neither!"

"Then what I am?"

"A boy who thinks he's a man."

Leung slapped his uncle's finger away. "I don't need your permission."

"Yes, you do. I made a promise to your father, that I'd teach you to fight, I'd teach you to be a man. Unlike a board or a bone, a promise, once broken, can never be repaired. You don't need permission; you need patience."

"I know how to strike and how to defend myself. What more is there to learn?" Leung asked.

Uncle Tso reached for a wet towel. "As I said, patience."

Leung scowled. "Does that work with the fan-tan man at your gambling places?"

"Gambling is skill and luck," Tso said. "Fighting is skill, luck, and timing. Soon, both of us will know when the time is right to fight, and within the fight, when it is time to win."

CHAPTER SIX

"Who do you think is going to win?" Sean asked Leung.

For the third night in a row, they watched the fights at the Woodrat from a crack in the floor. Because it was Saturday, three fights were scheduled. Sean's father won his match, much to the displeasure of the crowd. The onlookers yelled and threw things into the fighters' circle after he dispatched his foe, another Irishman, in two rounds.

Leung knew he could beat any of them. Except for Sean's father, most of these men fought without skill, just brute strength. Most just used their knuckles to strike, ignoring the power of the palm blow.

Before the next battle started, a man cleared onlookers off the painted line that marked the fighters' circle, then stood between the fighters.

"That's Oakley," Sean explained. "Once a fighter is knocked down, he's got to get up before Oakley counts to ten. If not, then the fight's over."

Leung scratched his forehead. While he still wore the hat to cross over from Mott Street, he took it off once he and Sean were above the Woodrat. "Why?"

"*Why* what?" This was the first night Leung had dared to ask questions.

"Why ten?"

"Because those are the rules."

Leung knew the word, but it didn't make any sense to him. Fighting didn't have rules. When men fought for real, they fought to the death. When men fought for sport, they battled until one could fight no more. No rules were needed in the martial arts; there was honor instead.

"Although I heard there are some other rules out there," Sean said. "Some places, they make the fighters wear gloves. Gloves!"

Sean laughed. Leung wasn't sure why, but he laughed along with him.

"At a Woodrat fight, you can't hit a guy when he's down or pull his hair," Sean explained. "It's not just about protecting the fighters. The crowd too. Nobody wants to pay to see a dirty fight."

"Pay?"

"People pay money to see the fights. The fighters get some, and Lew Mayflower, the guy who runs the Woodrat, gets more. That's what my pops says. But the people who make the real money are the gamblers. You get odds and pick a winner."

Leung asked more questions about things he'd seen but not understood. The more Sean talked, the more confused Leung became.

"So, you want to bet on the next fight?" Sean asked. "I'll take the kid. How much money you got?"

Leung shook his head. Other than Uncle Tso, nobody in their neighborhood had money. And Tso either had a lot or very little, depending on his luck that week.

"If my guy wins, you take me to Chinatown. I hear the food is fine, and I'm starved. If your guy wins—"

"If my guy wins," Leung said, "then we fight each other." Perfect form came not only from practice but from the testing of one's skills.

CHAPTER SEVEN

"Gentlemen, are you ready for the main event?"

The man's gravelly voice traveled all the way to Leung's hiding spot. Leung knew he'd need to watch this next fight even more carefully since, one fight earlier, he'd won his bet. Soon he'd battle Sean. His first time boxing would not be against an enemy but against someone who might become his friend.

"Who is that?" Leung asked Sean, pointing at the man in the middle of the circle.

"That's Mr. Mayflower," Sean answered.

The two fighters below looked like brutes, especially the larger man with the handlebar mustache. Tattoos covered the man's body, including a bald eagle across his shoulders.

"In this corner, from the Five Points by way of the Emerald Isle, Michael O'Reilly."

The crowd booed more than it cheered, just like when Sean's father had fought.

"And in this corner, the Warrior from Wall Street, Douglas Truman!" The floor seemed to shake beneath Leung, so loud and long were the cheers for the tattooed, mustached man.

"Truman's never lost, but then again, he's never fought my father," Sean said. He slapped Leung lightly on the back.

After Oakley yelled, "Fight!" the battle began. Blows came hard and heavy, mostly Truman's fists against O'Reilly's face.

"It's a mismatch, but that's what the crowd wants, so Mayflower gives it to them."

"Don't they want a good fight?" Leung asked. He'd never heard the word mismatch, but he knew the fighters below lacked discipline.

Truman was neither snake nor crane. He was like a dragon—so big and strong that he could do whatever he wanted.

"No," Sean said.

"Then what do they want?"

"Irish blood," Sean said softly. O'Reilly fell after a haymaker from the tattooed man.

Leung watched as O'Reilly put up his fists once more to box with Truman. Truman seemed to be smiling. Leung didn't understand why O'Reilly didn't try another approach. In Wing Chun, you found a foe's strength and used it against him. You found his weakness too. Truman was strong but slow. He'd lose to a trained Wing Chun fighter.

With an uppercut, Truman launched O'Reilly like a cannonball across the Woodrat floor. As O'Reilly crashed down, a roar went up from the crowd.

"When he wakes up, we'll learn what kind of man this O'Reilly bloke is," Sean said.

"We just saw that," Leung said.

Sean put his hand on Leung's shoulder. "No, we saw what kind of fighter he was. Not very tough or experienced. What he decides to do after the fight tells us more about him."

Leung understood the words, but not what Sean meant by them. "Decides to do?"

Sean grinned. "Let's see what O'Reilly decides to pick up first. His money or his teeth."

CHAPTER EIGHT

"Where is Uncle Tso?" Leung asked. It was the second most important question of the day. Once he found Tso, he'd ask the first: for permission to fight Sean.

Uncle Nang sipped his tea, shook his head, and pointed south down Mott. North on Mott was were where men worked in laundries or made cigars. South was where they went to gamble.

Leung had never understood how two brothers could be so different. Nang was smart and steady, while Tso knew fighting and fan-tan. In fan-tan, a banker emptied a handful of small objects onto a table, then covered them with a bowl. As the banker removed objects from under the bowl, four at a time, Tso and other gamblers wagered how many objects would be left. Like fighting, fan-tan demanded skill and luck. Yet in its way, fan-tan was more dangerous. Gamblers weren't concerned about honor when settling debts.

"When will he be back?" Leung asked. Another sip, another head shake from Nang.

Leung's father had stood somewhere between his oldest brother, Nang, and his youngest, Tso. He had put his intelligence not toward learning English nor toward gambling games, but only toward Wing Chun.

"Where have you been? Where did you sneak out to last night?" Nang asked. He didn't sound angry, only concerned. "We promised your father we'd watch after you."

Leung hung his head in shame. He wondered if his father would approve of his urge to fight outside of Chinatown. If Leung's father had been given a fair chance, Leung knew he could have bested any white man, even a bully like Truman. Leung didn't want to lie to his uncle, but he feared telling him the truth, so he said nothing. His uncle repeated the question, this time in Chinese, demanding an answer. An honest answer.

"The Woodrat." Leung explained about the fights he'd seen and how he wanted to fight. "This would make my father proud. It would honor his memory."

"I don't approve. Nothing good can come of it."

"I want to prove to them all that we're not weak."

"One man—one boy—doesn't stand for all of us."

Leung stood next to his uncle. He was half the man's age but at least a foot taller. "I can."

"Then look where it got your father," Uncle Nang said, tears under his words.

In his best English, hoping to make his uncle proud, Leung explained that Uncle Tso wouldn't let him fight until his form was perfect.

"How will I know when it is time?"

Uncle Nang didn't answer. Leung knew that Nang had never watched Leung's father or Uncle Tso fight. Nang always told them that Wing Chun was a waste of time. Leung's father would argue back that the martial arts built character as much as they did calluses.

"There is only one way to know anything, and that is to do it," Leung said. "Let me fight."

"Tso promised your father," Uncle Nang started.

"But you're the elder. Your words matter more," Leung argued back.

Uncle Nang rose from the wooden crate on which he sat. "Tso only listens to the fan-tan man saying 'one more game.'"

"Then you be my second," Leung said. He quickly explained some of the rules he'd learned from watching fights and listening to Sean. "If I lose, I won't ask to fight again."

Nang laughed, a broad laugh that Leung had not heard in a long time. "You sound like Tso, making promises that you can't keep. Just one more game, just one game."

"It's not gambling when you know you're going to win," Leung said. He threw a swift front kick, shattering the wood crate that Uncle Nang had been sitting on. "Maybe my form isn't perfect, but my desire to win is."

CHAPTER NINE

"Where's your second?" Sean asked. Sean's father stood behind him.

Leung said nothing. He thought Uncle Nang had agreed to be in his corner, but when Leung had left Mott Street in the twilight, Nang was nowhere to be found.

"Do you still want to do this?" Sean asked. Leung wondered if Sean was asking out of worry for Leung or for his own safety.

Leung nodded and tossed his hat to the

ground. Either Sean or Sean's father had drawn a chalk circle in vacant area just outside the Five Points. Leung almost got lost more than on his way there, but he made it in time.

He'd been more afraid of the journey than the fight. He knew that was good sign. Uncle Nang's absence was not. An hour before leaving, Leung had left a map that Sean had drawn under his uncle's teacup. Under the map, Leung wrote the Chinese characters for twilight. Just before he started his journey, Leung saw the map had vanished. Was Nang lost?

"This is my father, Sheamus Murphy," Sean said.

Leung bowed, then accepted the older man's hand.

"I told my dad you didn't know all the rules," Sean continued.

"These are the rules for *real* boxing. None of that gloved stuff," Mr. Murphy said. Leung couldn't follow most of what he was being told. Mr. Murphy talked quicker than Sean, with a heavy accent. Leung thought he should ask the man to slow down or to let Sean explain, but he didn't want to seem like a fool.

"I hafta say, you don't have a Chinaman's chance," Mr. Murphy added, then laughed way too loud. Leung hated that expression, and he decided to let Sean's dad know it.

"Don't say that!" Leung shouted.

Sean's dad folded his arms, amused.

Leung struggled to remain calm. Relax. Breathe. Balance.

"My dad's just teasing you, trying to get under your skin," Sean said. "Look, when I told him about you, I didn't think he'd like it one bit, but what did you say, Dad?"

"Both the Irish and Chinese are used to get kicked around, so we'd better learn to fight back. But if you're gonna fight, do it the right way. You understand, fella?" Mr. Murphy asked.

Leung nodded and walked toward the circle's rim. On the opposite side, Sean and his father talked. Impatient, Leung began to practice his form, like Uncle Tso had taught him.

Sean and his father walked toward the center. "Now, boys, I know you want to fight, but let's not get carried away," Mr. Murphy said. "I don't want anybody hurt. If it looks like it's going that way, I'm going to stop it. Understand?"

Leung nodded, then stripped off his shirt. Sean did the same. Sean's skin was pale. His arms were long but not muscled. Leung felt confident he could win.

"I also don't want to be here all night, so after ten rounds, we say it's a draw," Mr. Murphy added.

Leung hid his smile. The fight wouldn't last ten rounds. It wouldn't last ten minutes. While Leung had seen bareknuckle boxers before, he knew Sean had never seen a Wing Chun fighter. Sean had two fists. Leung had eight weapons: fist, elbow, knee, and foot, both left and right. He didn't need Nang's abacus to know which sum was greater.

"You ready?" Sean asked. Leung nodded again, and they both took up fighting stances.

Leung let the fresh twilight air work its way through his body, from his lungs to his fists, elbows, knees, and feet. He was centered, relaxed, balanced.

As Leung moved toward Sean, he felt a sharp pain. Not from a fist to the face but from a bamboo rod smacking against the back of his legs.

CHAPTER TEN

"What are you doing here?" Uncle Tso shouted.

Leung hung his head in shame. Anger at Uncle Tso rose within him and destroyed his centered calm.

He didn't answer Uncle Tso; no words in English or Chinese mattered.

"Answer me!" The bamboo rod almost split against Leung's shins.

"Is there a problem, fella?" Sean's father yelled. Leung motioned for him to stay back.

Sean put his shirt on and went back to his corner.

In his right hand, Tso held the map that Leung had left for Nang.

"I told your father that I wouldn't let you fight . . ."

Leung blocked the words, just as he blocked out the pain of the rod cracking against his ankles. He remembered the scene of Tso's promise like it was yesterday and in front of him, not five years ago and thousands of miles away.

After the riot in California, everyone was hurt. Many were dead, but more would have died if Leung's father hadn't fought back. He had dispatched one rioter after another to protect Leung, the other children, and the few women. It was the most honorable act: sacrificing yourself to protect others.

But even perfect form, the essence of the crane and the snake, was no match for weapons. Leung's father fought them off with his bamboo stick, but there were too many.

After a time, the rioters left. Not because the police had arrived—some of the police had even taken part—but because there was no more damage to do. The wounded immigrants gathered together. The herbs and oils that Nang used to cure so many things couldn't stop the blood oozing from the wounds of Leung's father. As he lay taking his last breaths, he told Tso to make Leung a Wing Chun fighter with perfect form, so perfect that no man dared challenge him. Tso promised on his life.

As Leung recalled the scene, he remembered another promise that Tso made to his brother: to stop gambling. Tso had broken it a hundred times since they'd arrived in New York. Uncle Tso was an honorable man humbled by a bad habit. Leung would use his uncle's weakness against him—just as Tso had taught him.

He grabbed the rod out of his uncle's hands, then stood surprised at how easily Tso had let it go. Tso's eyes flared, but he said nothing.

"How much?" Leung asked. His uncle didn't answer. Instead he reached for the bamboo rod. It was then that Leung noticed his uncle's hands. They were damaged, permanently, from railroad work, although Tso could still use them to spar and gamble. Leung had sensed that Tso's gambling debts were large, but he'd never realized that Tso had made a down payment with the top of his left ring finger.

"Come with me," Leung said. His uncle followed, more like a child than an adult.

Sean stopped them. "So, are we fighting or not?"

Leung nodded. "Yes. I have my second now. But there's one thing we forgot."

Leung whispered in Tso's ear, then handed him back the bamboo rod. Uncle Tso took the rod in his right hand, but he didn't raise it against Leung. Instead, Tso began to draw something in the dirt.

"Like you said, Sean, I'm no fool," Leung said.

Sean and his father stared at the symbol that Uncle Tso had sketched: a dollar sign.

CHAPTER ELEVEN

"Are you sure, Leung?" Uncle Tso asked. Leung nodded one last time and then walked slowly toward the center of the circle. He needed to fight to prove himself; his uncle needed the money to save himself. Maybe a promise was like bamboo; it could bend without breaking.

"Fight!" Mr. Murphy yelled.

Sean and Leung stared at each other until Sean smiled.

Like the boxers Leung had seen at the

Woodrat, Sean started to throw punches at Leung's face. Where the bareknuckle brutes would block the swings with their elbows, Leung swatted them away with his palms. Sean backed away as if he couldn't believe what he had seen.

Leung closed the distance, waiting to strike. Sean attacked again, throwing the same punches: right jab, left hook, another jab. None landed with any force, nor knocked Leung off balance. Wing Chun taught that striking with the closed fist wasted energy and channeled tension—but Sean wouldn't have known that.

For a third time, Leung let Sean throw punches, mostly hard jabs. Unable to strike, Sean tried to push Leung over, but Leung knocked him back with two hard palm blows to the chin.

"You slap like a girl," Sean said. He stepped up and threw a wild hook, which missed and sent him off balance. Leung stayed centered and slammed his open palm into Sean's nose.

Sean appeared angry and scared as blood trickled down his face.

Like vultures on a dead animal, a swarm of palm blows smacked against the side of Sean's face. As Sean put his hands up, Leung attacked with five, ten, and then fifteen rapid-fire punches, each one landing between Sean's eyes. Sean tried to defend himself, but Leung closed in. Standing on his left leg, Leung pivoted and unleashed the power of his right leg with a side kick. The energy surged from Leung's hip to knee to foot and smashed into Sean's side.

"No kicking!" Leung heard Mr. Murphy shout. Sean started to fall. As Sean tumbled, Leung landed a centerline punch to his opponent's jaw that caused Sean's eyes to roll back in his head. Mr. Murphy didn't even bother to count, tending to his son instead.

"Is he okay?" Leung asked as he followed behind Mr. Murphy. Sean struggled to his feet.

"He'll be okay, but you won't if you do that again, fella," Mr. Murphy said. "Kicking is against the rules. So you beat him, but you lose for breaking the rules."

Leung accepted Mr. Murphy's words. His concern was for Sean's well-being.

"Heck of a fight," Sean finally said. He tried to shake Leung's hand, but had a hard time finding it with his eyes swelling shut. "I don't know what that was, but it wasn't boxing."

"Whatever it was, I gotta admit, it sure worked," Mr. Murphy said. "You know, Leung, with some more training, you might have the makings of champion."

"Could I fight at the Woodrat?" Leung asked.

"You have nothing to prove," Leung's uncle snapped. "Let's go home."

"My uncle says no," Leung said. He didn't try to hide the disappointment in his voice.

"What would make him change his mind?" Mr. Murphy asked. Leung pointed at the dollar sign, still perfectly etched in the dirt behind them.

CHAPTER TWELVE

"Sean, what's wrong?" Leung asked.

The noise below them at the Saturday night fight was growing louder, and Sean had told Leung that his ears still rang from their fight a few days ago. Leung suspected something else—that Sean was worried about his dad's fight.

"Sean, what's wrong?" he asked again. Sean still didn't answer. Originally, Sean's father had been scheduled to fight during the day. But then

Oakley told—not asked, but told—Mr. Murphy that he'd fight at night. He wouldn't be battling fellow Irishman Michael O'Reilly as planned. Instead, he'd box against Douglas Truman.

Leung started to speak again, but Sean waved his hand. He heard Oakley giving introductions. As before, there were few cheers when Oakley introduced Mr. Murphy—and more hisses than in a snake pit. Truman decided to introduce himself.

"I stand here before you the undefeated and uncrowned king of bareknuckle boxing in New York City. I've already defeated the papist O'Reilly, and in a few moments, I'll defeat another. When will a real American stand up and try to defeat me? Only then can I declare myself to be a true champion of this fine city, now infested with this foreign vermin."

The crowd cheered their approval and clapped in anticipation of the battle. Leung noticed some object with beads wrapped tight around Sean's hand. Sean spoke a few words under his breath and then kissed the beads as Mayflower yelled for the fight to start.

Both men assumed a fighting stance, yet for a good minute, they didn't touch each other. The crowd booed until Truman scored a hard jab to Mr. Murphy's jaw. Sean's dad fought off the blow, but he couldn't counter. Murphy's strikes were hard and fast but not accurate. An attempt at a hook left him off balance, and Truman took control with a blow from the right. A centered fighter could've blocked the punch easily, but Mr. Murphy stood no chance.

Round after round after round, the results were the same. Truman used his size and strength to absorb the punches Mr. Murphy got through, and he fought back with looping blows. Most of them didn't land, but the few that connected knocked Sean's father down and ended the round.

"Stay down," Leung heard Sean whisper. "Stay down, Dad, stay down."

Mr. Murphy couldn't hear Sean, and even if he could've, Leung guessed he wouldn't have listened. By the tenth round, Truman appeared to be tiring. Blood dribbled from the face of Mr. Murphy, but his breathing was steady. He'd weathered the storm.

Sean's father danced around the fighters' circle, making Truman chase him. The crowd booed, but it was the perfect strategy. Mr. Murphy used his brain and his brawn. Maybe he would tire the bigger man out, take all the energy out of his body, and then, when the time was right, strike.

Truman finally landed a jab, but instead of following up with another blow, he tied up Mr. Murphy's arms, not allowing him to punch. The two men looked more like dancers than fighters, and the crowd began to boo. Sean's father tried to push away, but he couldn't escape Truman's grip.

"He's going to win," Sean said, but then it happened. Truman bullied Mr. Murphy down to the ground. As they fell, Truman drove his knee into his foe's groin. Truman crawled to his feet while Sean's father lay in agony on the ground.

Sean's dad was face down when Oakley raised Truman's hand in the air. Truman walked over his fallen foe, toward the corner where a green handkerchief was tied to a nearby pole.

"That's the colors. The winner gets it," Sean said. "Like taking the flag of a nation you've defeated."

Truman held the handkerchief in the air, then blew his nose on it as the crowd roared.

CHAPTER THIRTEEN

"How did you find us?" Leung asked Sean and Mr. Murphy.

Amazingly, the Irishmen stood in the alley where Leung had been practicing centerline strikes on the wooden dummy. Sean's father's face looked like the American flag: red hair, white skin, and blue bruises.

"I just kept saying Wing Chun to everybody. That was enough," Sean said.

Both Sean and Leung laughed, although

Mr. Murphy's jaw didn't move.

"Sorry about your fight," Leung whispered to Mr. Murphy, then bowed in respect. Leung thought it took a tough man to take that kind of beating, to keep getting up only to be knocked down again. Only one kind of man was tougher: the one that never got knocked down at all.

"I think my dad should fight that cheater Truman again," Sean said. "He had him beat."

Leung nodded in agreement. "It is no shame to lose to a dishonorable man."

"But Dad doesn't want a rematch. He's got another idea," Sean said. "I don't agree, but you don't get anywhere arguing with your elders, right?"

Leung nodded, although he wasn't so sure. Just as his father had balanced between his brothers, Leung felt that he too was stuck in the middle, with each uncle trying to pull him toward the older man's way of life. But the key to life was to stay centered.

"I suppose you're wondering what we're doing here," Sean continued.

Mr. Murphy sat on Uncle Tso's wooden stool. It wasn't warm, since Leung's uncle had not been seen in days. Leung wondered if Tso was celebrating a big gambling win or running from another loss. Would he come home with gold rings on every finger or one less knuckle on his left hand?

"What's that?" Mr. Murphy managed to say as he pointed at the wooden dummy.

Leung was more than happy to show off the form exercises. Sean and his father marveled as Leung threw strikes at the dummy.

Afterward, Leung explained as best he could how the three arms and one leg of the dummy represented a foe's positions and the lines of force. The dummy was mounted on slats to resemble a human's way of absorbing energy.

"Master the dummy, master the man," Leung said with pride.

"It's not the same as sparring with a real person, though, is it?" Sean asked.

"No, but it helps me develop perfect form," Leung answered.

Sean raised an eyebrow. "I don't think you can become a real boxer without fighting against someone."

"No one else here in the Five Points excels at Wing Chun," Leung explained. "And no one knows how to box."

"But I know how to box, and—" Sean started to say.

Leung shook his head. "We could not be friends if we fought all the time."

Sean laughed and patted Leung's shoulder. "That's true, but to be honest, I don't think I want to fight you again. I thought I could box, but there's no way I could ever beat you."

Leung bowed in respect and in thanks.

"How about me?" Mr. Murphy said softly.

Leung's head snapped back. "You?"

"The only way to beat Truman is to become the best fighter possible," Sean said.

Leung nodded his head. "Of course, but I thought . . ."

"I said that my dad didn't want a rematch," Sean continued. "And that's right."

"Then . . . ?"

"You," Mr. Murphy said. He tried his best to smile.

"Me?" Leung asked.

"My dad thinks that with training, you could defeat Truman. So, how about it, fella?"

CHAPTER FOURTEEN

"So that's it. Do I have your permission?"

Leung couldn't bring himself to make eye contact with Uncle Tso or Uncle Nang. The three sat in the alley, away from the stifling heat of the crowded tenement. As Leung had explained what Mr. Murphy proposed, he sensed anger and suspicion growing within his uncles.

Nang and Tso sipped their tea, but neither spoke, each man waiting for the other, almost like the start of a fight.

"I have to tell them today," Leung said. Mr. Murphy had learned about a day of fights scheduled for the Fourth of July, two months away. Leung would need to train and get in at least one fight to be included.

"I want to talk with these people," Uncle Nang finally said.

Tso said nothing, just sipped his tea. He didn't admit to having met the Murphys.

"I am torn," Nang said, speaking in Chinese so Tso could understand. "We're never invited into the white world, except to feed or entertain them. But with this, you could get hurt, Leung. Yet, you could also show the toughness of the Chinese people."

Tso spoke: "He will show them nothing of the kind. He cannot win. His form is not yet perfect. He can defend, but he cannot attack. He lacks perspective and patience."

Leung hung his head in shame. His uncle did not believe in him. Part of him wanted to say, "Maybe the teacher, not the student, is to blame." But he stayed silent.

"Win or lose, you could be hurt," Nang said.

"We've had enough pain in our family."

"But I will win, I will show them, and I will bring pain, not take it," Leung said. He knew Tso was right; his form was not yet perfect, and it would never be. He would never be as skilled in Wing Chun as his father had been or as skilled as Tso wanted him to be. He'd be something else instead: someone who could take Wing Chun to victory in bareknuckle boxing.

Tso took his right finger and poked Leung in the chest. "No good can come of this. Maybe, when you are older, and your form is—"

"They pay fighters," Leung said. "I would give the money to you, my teacher."

Another chest poke, this one not as hard. "How much?" Tso asked.

Before Leung could answer, Uncle Nang knocked Tso's finger away. "Whatever you would earn, Leung, you keep. For you, Tso, it would not be enough."

"I need your permission, Uncle Nang. You are the elder," Leung said.

Nang stared at his brother. "I will let Tso decide. It was he who made the promise."

Uncle Tso stood and started to leave. "There is nothing to decide. I have said that—"

Leung called after his uncle: "The real money, I understand, is from the gambling on the fights."

Tso turned around. "They bet?"

Leung nodded while Nang sighed deeply.

"No one would expect me to win, so the odds would be against me. Someone betting on me could make a lot of money."

"Perhaps . . . one fight," Tso said softly. Then he began to ask questions about the betting.

Leung explained what little he knew. Tso smiled, nodded, and soaked up the information like a sponge.

"So I have your permission?" Leung asked. Tso nodded. His left hand emerged from his pocket as he absently held his tea, revealing one thumb, three fingers, and one stump.

CHAPTER FIFTEEN

"Are you ready for the hard part?"

Drenched in sweat, Leung stared in confusion at Mr. Murphy. Murphy had spent the last four hours teaching Leung the basics of bareknuckle boxing. All the while, Leung had struggled to maintain Wing Chun practices. Leung wondered what the man meant by his remark. What could be harder?

"We need to sell the idea to Mr. Mayflower," Mr. Murphy said. "Let's get cleaned up."

Mr. Murphy dipped a towel in a bucket of water and tossed it to Leung. He dipped another one for himself. Sweat and hard work knew no nation.

Like Uncle Tso, Mr. Murphy was a natural teacher. Sometimes, down by the docks where they trained, Murphy would fight with Leung. Other times, he'd have Leung and Sean spar. All the while, he'd stop, explain the mistake Leung had made, and make Leung perform the move until he got it right. It was done at half speed so no one got hurt, but it was as tough as any training that Uncle Tso had ever put Leung through. Unlike Tso, whose training was about perfect form, Mr. Murphy focused on practical fighting: skills and strategies. With luck, they'd mix the best of the bareknuckle boxing style with Wing Chun to create a new fighting form.

"Put your hat on," Mr. Murphy said. Leung did as he was told. As they walked from the abandoned field through the crowded streets toward Woodrats, not a word was said by Leung or the Murphys. Nor by the people they passed who, had they noticed, would have been shocked at the sight of a Chinese boy, outside of Chinatown, walking with two Irishmen.

Once they arrived at the Woodrat, Mr. Murphy told Sean and Leung to wait in the alley. But no sooner had Mr. Murphy left than Sean motioned for Leung to follow him to their watching spot. Leung wanted to hear the men talk, but more than that, he wanted to leave the stinking alley.

Even though no fight was taking place, it was loud inside the Woodrat. But then again, it was always loud in the Bowery. Sometimes the noise of so many people in such a small space reminded Leung of the roar of locomotive. Except most of these people were going nowhere, trapped in tenement slums—unless they took a gamble at getting out.

Trying to ignore the noise, Leung watched as Lew Mayflower yelled at Sean's dad. Mr. Murphy didn't yell back. Instead, he laughed and whispered something to Mayflower. Mayflower nodded, and then the two men started to walk toward the back door, to the alley. A heavy drunk stumbled alongside them, wrapped in a headlock by Oakley.

Quickly, Leung and Sean returned to the alley. Seconds later, Lew Mayflower, Murphy, Oakley, and the drunk emerged. "That's him," Mr. Murphy said. "Show him something, Leung."

Leung looked at Mr. Murphy, unsure what the man wanted. Mayflower put money in the hand of the drunk and then pushed him toward Leung. "Fight that boy!" Mayflower yelled.

The drunk put the money in his pants, stripped off his shirt, and assumed a fighting pose. Leung did the same.

"Lose the hat, kid," Mayflower said. With great reluctance, Leung removed his hat. His bald head shone in the heat, while the long dark hair swayed behind him. The drunk threw the first punch, a hard left that Leung deflected, as he did the next one and the one after that.

"Pretty good, huh, Mr. Mayflower?" Mr. Murphy said.

Blocking the punches was easy for Leung. Trying to restrain from kicking was harder. He'd lift his leg for a front kick and pull back. Leung saw that when he did that, the drunk leaned backwards, off balance. It was the opening he needed. Leung drove straight-line punches to the man's face.

CHAPTER SIXTEEN

"Any questions?" Mr. Murphy asked Uncle Nang.

Nang shook his head and then spoke in Chinese to Tso. Like Leung, the two men hid their faces under their hats. Tso whispered something back to Nang.

"My brother wants to know if we will be allowed to watch the fight," Nang asked. Leung knew better. Tso didn't just want to watch the fight, he wanted to bet on it.

"I'll ask Mayflower," Mr. Murphy answered. "But on a rough night, it might not be the safest place . . ."

All Leung had told his uncles was that he'd be fighting at the Woodrat. He certainly didn't want to tell them about the fight in the alley or about the conversation afterward between Lew Mayflower and Sean's father. Even after Leung showed off his skills, Mayflower wasn't sure he wanted to book him for a Woodrat fight. He agreed only when Mr. Murphy pushed the idea that if Leung won, the victory would make him a contender to fight Douglas Truman, a fight many people would pay to see.

Leung tried to focus on his training. Mr. Murphy had adopted Lew Mayflower's training strategy for Leung. He'd recruit men from the alley behind Woodrats, sober them up with coffee, and pay them to spar with Leung. Few men lasted more than two rounds before ending up as Mr. Murphy had found them: face down in the dirt.

"Leung, attack the body," Mr. Murphy shouted. Leung nodded and waited for his chance. His hands were hurting. He had knocked out every opponent with his punches and palm blows, but the crunch of bone against bone shot pain through his arms. He had more and more trouble relaxing and staying able to uncoil a perfect strike.

The fighter across from him wore an eye patch over his left eye and had scars across his body. He might have fought in the war that started around the time that Leung arrived in California, the one between the North and the South. Many of the men Leung had seen in the Bowery's alleyways or drunk in the streets were missing body parts.

"Come on, fight!" Tso yelled in Chinese, which seemed to distract Leung's foe.

At first, Leung hadn't wanted to spar with these men. It didn't seem right. But he guessed the money Mr. Murphy gave them might be all they would earn that week.

When the man tried to fight up close, Leung ducked under his arms. He elbowed the man's ribs. As the man dropped his head in pain, Leung exploded with an uppercut that knocked the man down and out.

Leung looked around him. Uncle Tso, Mr. Murphy, and Sean were all smiles, but Uncle Nang's expression remained stoic. It was hard for Leung to know what Nang was thinking. The three other men Mr. Murphy had recruited were easy to read, even from a distance: the open eyes, clenched fists, and frowns revealed their fear.

"Who's next?" Sean yelled, but the men sat unmoving.

"Do you know who I'm fighting at the Woodrat?" Leung asked Sean as they waited for the next fighter to gather his courage. All Leung had been told was that he would fight in two weeks, on Saturday the second.

"He didn't tell you?" Sean said in a hard whisper. "You're fighting my dad."

CHAPTER SEVENTEEN

"Are you ready?" Nang asked Leung.

Leung nodded, took a deep breath, and bowed to his uncles. The three stood in the Woodrat's damp basement. Despite Tso's pride, he and Nang had agreed they'd be safest away from the rowdy crowd. They could hear the fight above, but Leung knew they wouldn't be able to see it, which he didn't mind. He knew he would win—but if he somehow lost, he couldn't stand to shame himself in front of his uncles.

As Leung walked to the fighters' circle, he heard people yelling at him. When his name was called, Leung took his hat off, and the on-lookers exploded in louder jeers. Leung couldn't understand most of the words they were yelling at him, which he thought was for the best. May-flower had paid one of his bouncers to act as Leung's second. The man didn't seem pleased.

When Mr. Murphy came to the circle, with Sean behind him as his second, the crowd met them with the same mix of boos and cheers. Leung knew that many visitors to the Woodrat hated the Irish almost as much as the Chinese. They probably didn't care who won; they just enjoyed watching the newcomers to their city beat each other up.

Oakley acted as the referee. He wished both fighters good luck, stepped out of the way, and yelled, "Fight!"

As always, Leung let his foe strike first. He'd sparred with Mr. Murphy enough to know the man's strengths, which were many, and his weaknesses, which were fewer—but Leung only needed one. Like Sean, once Mr. Murphy got angry, he threw wild punches, looking for a knock out. In Wing Chun, nothing was wild; everything was balanced.

The crowd cheered as Mr. Murphy threw the starting punch. When Leung countered, they jeered. But as the fight went on, the crowd grew quieter, stunned by Leung's hybrid style.

Leung waited patiently for an opening. An attempted left hook left Mr. Murphy off balance. Leung fought the urge to kick Murphy's leg. Instead, he put his own legs quickly behind Murphy and pushed him backward, tripping him. The crowd booed as Mr. Murphy hit the ground.

Oakley began to count, but only reached three before Mr. Murphy stood back up. The second round ended the same way, less than a minute later, with Leung knocking Murphy off balance and forcing him down with a palm strike.

Mr. Murphy tried fighting close in, locking up Leung's arms, but Leung remained centered. Murphy broke the grip and threw a short right to Leung's nose, then a left toward his stomach.

The left never landed, while the space between Murphy's hands created an opening that seemed to Leung wider than the ocean.

Leung struck with his palm to the jaw and a right fist to the temple. Alone, the strikes were not enough to knock a man out, no more than drops in a puddle. But thirty strikes in under a minute became a rainstorm of damage. Mr. Murphy toppled face first in front of Leung, and Oakley counted to ten.

Leung left the fighters' circle quickly as the crowd pelted him with garbage and slurs.

"You won," Nang said when Leung joined them in the closet. "I could tell."

Leung began describing the fight to his uncles, but Tso seemed distracted. A knock at the door interrupted their talk. It was Lew Mayflower.

"Here you go," Mayflower said.

Mayflower put a single bill in Leung's left hand, damp from his sweat and Murphy's blood. "And here's yours," Mayflower added as he placed a stack of bills in Tso's right hand.

CHAPTER EIGHTEEN

"So, what do you think?" Lew Mayflower asked Uncle Nang. Nang glanced at the single sheet of paper that McManus had handed him and then stared hard at Mayflower. Nang crumbled the paper and tossed it at Mayflower's feet.

"Maybe your brother might think differently," Mayflower said. He bent over to pick up the paper, but Nang put his foot over it.

"This will sell tickets," Mayflower said. Nang ground the paper with the heel of his sandal.

"What are you talking about?" Leung asked. His uncles, Sean and his father, and Mayflower stood in the backroom of the Woodrat. It was the first day of summer, hours before the club opened.

"I want you to fight Douglas Truman on the Fourth of July fight card," Mayflower explained.

"You've got to do it, Leung. It's a perfect chance," Mr. Murphy said.

"I'll pay double what I paid you last time," Mayflower said.

"Does my nephew get paid as much as Truman?" Nang asked.

Mayflower shook his head.

"Then why should he fight at all?" Nang asked.

Before he could answer, Uncle Tso began asking Nang questions. Nang explained what Mayflower had proposed. Tso laughed.

"What's so funny?" Mayflower asked.

"My brother doesn't agree that Leung's pay should double," Nang answered.

Leung frowned. Tso had made more on Leung's fight with Mr. Murphy than anyone else, and without taking a punch. This was probably some sort of lesson in humility.

"A wise man!" Mayflower said and then bowed, as if mocking Tso.

"Triple," Tso said, in English.

Leung and Nang appeared stunned by Tso's use of English. Maybe the man knew just enough to place bets. Money was a common language.

Tso motioned for Nang to come closer and then whispered in his ear. Leung couldn't hear them, but while they spoke, the hard look on Nang's face began to soften.

Nang faced Mayflower. "My brother says Leung gets paid as much as the other fighter, and—"

"Out of the question," Mayflower said. "If people found out that I paid a Chinaman as much as a white man, they'd never come back to the Woodrat. I'll give him double what he got last time. And if he should win, I'll give triple— but only we know about it. Agreed?"

Nang explained the terms to Tso, who nodded in agreement. Even head down under a hat,

Leung saw his uncle's smile.

"Those were my brother's conditions, now here are mine," Nang said.

Mayflower huffed like a steam engine. "What now?"

"We want our people to be able to see the fight, up front," Nang said. "If Leung is good enough to fight at Woodrats, then we are good enough to watch him. Guarantee our safety."

Mayflower looked at Mr. Murphy, who shrugged. "Okay, but I have a condition too," Mayflower said.

"What's that?" Nang asked.

Mayflower motioned for Nang to lift his foot, then picked up the sheet of paper.

"You have to help promote the fight and sell tickets," Mayflower said. He smoothed out the paper and handed it back to Uncle Nang. Nang touched it like it was diseased.

Leung ripped the paper from his uncle's hands. "Let me see!"

While Leung continued to improve speaking English, he still couldn't read the poster's words. But the pictures on the paper said it all.

There was Truman under an American flag, and Leung, or someone like him, but drawn to look evil, with horns coming out of his head and a pointed tail hanging down his back.

"The devil from the East meets the savior of the West on the Fourth of July!" McManus said. "What can I say? It'll pack 'em in."

The white men all laughed. Uncle Tso even joined in, but not Nang, and not Leung. Like the drawing, Uncle Nang's expression was easy to read: fear.

CHAPTER NINETEEN

"Who's first?" Mr. Murphy asked the stable of groggy looking men he'd recruited to spar with Leung at the Kung Wa Theater. Leung had been in the theater only a few times before, and certainly never on the stage where Murphy and Mayflower had put together a makeshift boxing ring.

None of the men stood up, which was fine with Leung. With the match against Truman one week away, Leung didn't think he needed to do these fights. And he wanted time to rest his hands. Even so, Mayflower had insisted that letting people watch him train would create more interest in the July match.

While Murphy poured coffee into a small man with heavily tattooed arms, Uncle Nang took the stage. Nang had refused to distribute the paper with the picture of Leung as a devil, but he kept his word and promoted the fight, letting Tso sell tickets. Nang commanded attention as he explained the rules to the mostly Chinese crowd. Leung watched the crowd react in surprise at all the things that were not allowed: strikes below the waist, tearing of the flesh, kicking, eye gouging, or striking a man when down. Many in the crowd began to laugh.

Just before the first fighter stood up, a commotion came from the back of the theater. Heads turned, and some people begin to head for the exits. Leung could see why: it was Douglas Truman, surrounded by a dozen policemen. The policemen waved their clubs, moving people out of the way so Truman could reach the stage.

Once onstage, Truman ripped off his shirt, flexed his muscles, and assumed a fighter's pose. At the foot of the stage, along with the police, were two men with a camera.

"Where's that Chinese boy who thinks he can defeat me?" Truman bellowed.

Leung refused to move. He'd meet Truman soon enough at the Woodrat, and then Leung knew he would be standing over the fallen fighter. That would deserve a photograph.

With Leung centered in place, Truman stomped toward him. Both of Leung's uncles stood in front of their nephew, while police stood behind Truman. Nang and Tso's instinct to protect Leung—to protect family—trumped reason or caution.

"Come on, boy. Give the press something. That's the Police Gazette boxing reporter!" Truman pointed at a small man with glasses who wrote in a small notebook. "Come Fourth of July, I will tame the devil!"

Truman shouted so loud, even people who'd fled the theater were likely to hear him. Next, he pushed Nang and Tso to the floor. Before

Leung could strike at the man, a group of policeman jumped between them.

Truman backed away, picked up his shirt, and made his way for the exit, tailed by the reporter, photographers, and policemen. Along the way, the police managed to do more that wave their clubs in the air; they connected against any Chinese onlookers in their path. The dull thud of clubs hitting skulls echoed not only in the theater but in Leung's memory.

Leung closed his eyes and recalled the night of the riot. The screams and the shouts as the mob, with the help of the police, ran down the Chinese. Homes burned, hundreds hurt, and a dozen dead. It was a massacre brought on by hatred and fear, the same emotions that Truman had shown on stage.

Once again, Leung had to find the center of the situation. If he lost, he proved that a white man was stronger than he was, and Tso would be in worse debt with the gamblers. If he won, he knew the end result: another riot, another massacre.

CHAPTER TWENTY

"Gentlemen, you know the rules. The fight ends when one of you cannot stand up before the ten count, if your second surrenders for you, or if you agree to a draw. Understood?" Leung struggled to hear Lew Mayflower over the roar of the massive crowd.

Leung's uncles were the only Chinese that he could see, even though he was told that all the tickets had been sold. Had the bouncers refused to allow them in? Did Mayflower go back on his word? Or did they stay away, fearing for their safety if Leung should win?

With Uncle Tso as his second and Nang has his bottle holder, Leung returned to his corner. Nang set down the bottle of water and tied a handkerchief to a pillar, as Mayflower had instructed.

"Don't bother to tie it tight," Leung told his uncle. "He won't be taking it. I will win this fight—for me, for all of us."

"Fight!" Mayflower yelled. The crowd roared in approval. Spectators seemed to push closer to the fighters' circle as one mass. The smell of alcohol, tobacco, and sweat filled the Woodrat. American flags hung around the circle as Leung, stripped of his shirt, relaxed his arms into perfect position.

Unlike Mr. Murphy or Leung's sparring partners, Truman didn't throw wild punches. Instead, he fought through Leung's defensive strikes and easily wrestled him to the ground. Although it was against the rules, Truman jammed a knee into Leung's side.

For the first time since he had started

training with Sean's father, Leung took the thirty seconds allotted between rounds to find his balance. After the rest, both fighters returned to the circle. Once again, Truman muscled his way pass Leung's lightning-quick strikes, tied up Leung's arms, and then threw him to the floor. This time the knee landed harder, catching Leung in the ribs. He gasped for breath.

The next five rounds ended the same way: a throw, an illegal blow, but with Leung standing before the ten count. After fighting both Truman and his own anger at Truman's dirty tricks, Leung was tired.

As round six began, Truman used his long reach to grab Leung's hair with his left hand and punch at him with his right. Leung blocked the punches with palm blows and waited for the older man to tire. The second Truman paused, Leung attacked. With his right hand, Leung chopped hard on Truman's left wrist, breaking the man's grip on his hair—and Truman's wrist. With his left palm, Leung fired blows across Truman's eyes.

The crowd jeered as Truman fell like an old

tree. Leung returned to his corner and watched as Truman crawled to his. At the end of the rest period, Truman pulled himself to his feet. He bled and breathed heavily.

"Fight!" Mayflower shouted.

And Leung did, blocking every punch, pushing back every attempt to tie him up, and using the growing time between Truman's attacks to launch his own strikes. He pounded not just at Truman's face but at the man's kidneys, time and time again. Blood soon oozed through the man's no-longer-smiling mouth.

While Truman had won the first six rounds, Leung dominated the next six. He threw accurate strikes that were too fast for the older man to counter. Truman was slow and getting slower. The crowd had grown quiet as Leung punished his beaten foe, but as the thirteenth round began, onlookers surged forward as if they were trying to prop Truman up. Truman made it up at the seven count. To Leung, it seemed as though Mayflower counted very slowly.

Three more times, Leung ended the round by knocking Truman down but not out. These rounds lasted longer than the earlier ones, as Truman had stopped punching. Leung sensed Truman had figured out Leung's strategy. Truman lunged at Leung, butting him in the stomach like a ram. As Leung fell backwards, he landed a hard palm blow to Truman's chin. The man's knees buckled. The round ended with both men down.

Leung bounced back to his feet, but Truman remained face down. Mayflower began the ten count. With each number, Leung sensed the count growing slower and the crowd getting closer, growing louder, preparing for outrage.

Leung could barely hear the count of "nine"—as the noise around him was louder than most any he'd heard before. Only once had he heard louder—at the riot that caused his family to flee California.

Mayflower opened his mouth, ready to count Truman out. Leung knew he must be like bamboo—firm by flexible. He stepped out of the fighters' circle, signaling his willingness to quit. Mayflower grabbed him. "That's against the rules. I could disqualify you."

Leung shook his head to indicate that he didn't understand.

"You'll lose for breaking the rules," Mayflower said. Leung looked over Mayflower's shoulder. Truman was on his knees, nowhere close to standing. The crowd inched in. Once more, the odds were against Leung's family.

Pushing past Mayflower, Leung used all his weapons against the cheating bully. Fist, elbow, and knee knocked Truman out. The crowd booed and pushed into the fighters' circle until Mayflower raised the hand of the fallen fighter. Truman's second took the colors from Leung's corner. It was official—Leung had been disqualified. In the chaos, Leung, Tso, and Nang escaped out the Woodrat's back exit.

"I'm sorry I lost," Leung said as they sprinted into the night, toward Mott Street. They ran so fast that Leung didn't take time to stop and ask, "Uncle Tso, why are you smiling?"

CHAPTER TWENTY-ONE

"Do it again," Uncle Tso instructed Leung. They worked in the alley with the wooden dummy. "Stay balanced!"

Leung nodded in agreement and delighted in showing off his form, the perfect kicks in particular. Uncle Tso said nothing. He sat, hands in his pockets, smiling.

It had been two days since Leung lost the fight.

Once Leung and Uncle Nang made it back to Chinatown, Tso had disappeared.

Lew Mayflower wanted Leung to fight Truman again, but Leung had refused. He had nothing to prove. The Woodrat had its rules, but Leung had his honor. Honor was better to have and easier to understand.

When Uncle Tso had returned to Chinatown after his disappearance, Leung whispered to him, "I'm sorry." He avoided looking at Tso. His uncle kept his hands in his pockets, and Leung feared the worst. "I've shamed us," Leung continued. "I won't fight again. I'm sorry you lost—"

"Quiet!" Uncle Tso said, then slowly took his hands from his pockets. On every finger was a gold ring. "I lost nothing, nor did you. Once you'd proven you were better, there was nothing else to prove. You lost to protect us, am I right?"

Leung nodded in agreement.

"I took the money I won off your first fight and used it to buy the tickets Mayflower gave us to sell," Tso said. "Then I resold those tickets at twice their value to all the people who wanted to see you lose. I don't know the language, but I understand money."

"But then you didn't lose it all on my fight?" Leung was confused.

"No, I won all the bets I placed," Uncle Tso said. "I bet that you'd lose."

"Lose?"

"Of course. Do you know why?" Uncle Tso asked. He slapped the bamboo rod at the ground. "Because your form is not perfect! Center yourself!"

ABOUT THE AUTHOR

Patrick Jones is the author of numerous novels for teens, including the Dojo series from Darby Creek, as well as the nonfiction books *The Main Event: The Moves and Muscle of Pro Wrestling* and *Ultimate Fighting: The Brains and Brawn of Mixed Martial Arts* for Millbrook Press. A former librarian for teenagers, he received a lifetime achievement award from the American Library Association in 2006. He lives in Minneapolis but still considers Flint, Michigan, his hometown. He can be found on the web at www.connectingya.com.

BARE KNUCKLE

NEW YORK CITY.
THE 1870s.
THE FIGHT STARTS NOW.

WELCOME TO THE DOJO

LEARN TO FIGHT,
LEARN TO LIVE,
AND LEARN
TO FIGHT
FOR YOUR
LIFE.